KIT'S TREE HOUSE

BY VALERIE TRIPP

ILLUSTRATIONS WALTER RANE

VIGNETTES RENÉE GRAEF, SUSAN MCALILEY

THE AMERICAN GIRLS COLLECTION®

Published by Pleasant Company Publications

For information, address: Book Editor, Pleasant Company Publications, 8400 Fairway Place, P.O. Box 620998, Middleton, WI 53562.

Visit our Web site at **americangirl.com**

Printed in Singapore.
03 04 05 06 07 08 09 TWP 10 9 8 7 6 5 4 3 2 1

Library of Congress Cataloging-in-Publication Data

Tripp, Valerie, 1951–
Kit's tree house / by Valerie Tripp ; illustrations, Walter Rane ; vignettes, Renée Graef, Susan McAliley.
p. cm. — (The American girls collection)
Summary: Ten-year-old Kit dreams of having a special tree house someday, but she is disappointed with the one her father and her friend build for her. Includes note on housing during the Depression and a related craft activity.

ISBN 1-58485-699-8
[1. Tree houses—Fiction. 2. Friendship—Fiction. 3. Depressions—1929—Fiction.]
I. Rane, Walter, ill. II. Title. III. Series.
PZ7.T7363 Kk 2003 [Fic]—dc21 2002029668

The AMERICAN GIRLS COLLECTION®

OTHER AMERICAN GIRLS
SHORT STORIES:

KAYA AND THE RIVER GIRL

THANKS TO JOSEFINA

KIRSTEN'S PROMISE

ADDY'S SUMMER PLACE

SAMANTHA'S SPECIAL TALENT

MOLLY'S PUPPY TALE

Picture Credits

The following organizations have generously given permission to reprint illustrations contained in "Looking Back": p. 34—J. C. Allen and Son; p. 36—Library of Congress; p. 38—Library of Congress; p. 39—Library of Congress; p. 40—Library of Congress; p. 41—© The Procter & Gamble Company. Used by permission.

Table of Contents

KIT'S FAMILY

DAD
Kit's father, a businessman facing the problems of the Great Depression.

MOTHER
Kit's mother, who takes care of her family and their home with strength and determination.

KIT
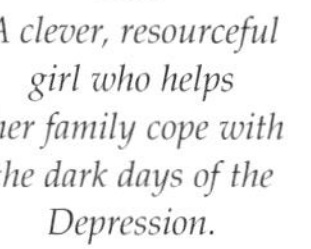

A clever, resourceful girl who helps her family cope with the dark days of the Depression.

CHARLIE
Kit's affectionate and supportive older brother.

AUNT MILLIE
The lively and loving woman who raised Dad.

. . . And Friends

Mrs. Howard
Mother's garden club friend, who is a guest in the Kittredge home.

Ruthie Smithens
Kit's best friend, who is loyal, understanding, and generous.

Stirling Howard
Mrs. Howard's son, whose delicate health hides surprising strengths.

Kit's Tree House

Kit Kittredge tilted her head back as far as it would go and looked up at the highest branches of the tree, which looked black and spidery against the blue sky. "You can really *see* a tree in the fall," she said to her friends Ruthie and Stirling, who were helping her rake leaves on a cold fall day. "You can really get to know a tree when its leaves are gone."

"You can really get to know the

leaves, too," teased Ruthie, tossing a handful at Kit. "Closely!"

Kit laughed as the leaves fluttered down around her and her dog, Grace. One leaf landed on Grace's head like a hat. "Wouldn't it be great," said Kit dreamily, "to have a tree house way up there?" She pointed up to the high branches. "You'd be on top of the world. You'd be able to see for miles."

"Sure," said Stirling.

But Ruthie said, "Are you crazy, Kit? Those high branches are too skinny to hold a tree house. The lower branches are bigger and stronger. And it wouldn't be so far to fall if your tree house should come crashing down

"Wouldn't it be great," said Kit dreamily, "to have a tree house way up there?"

someday. It would be much smarter to build lower."

"I guess you're right," said Kit. She slid her gaze down, down, down the tree trunk from the high-flying branches to the stout, solid lower branches. But, *boing,* somehow her gaze bounced right back up to the top of the tree. Kit grinned and went back to work, raking so energetically that the too-short sleeves of her old winter coat rode up and left her wrists bare to the cold. "Someday soon I'll have the tree house of my dreams," she said. "I'm determined."

Ruthie and Stirling smiled. They knew that Kit had wanted a tree house forever. She'd come close to having one about a year ago, when Ruthie's father had offered her wood left over from building a new garage. But Kit had generously sacrificed that wood so that Dad could turn the sleeping porch into a room that could be rented. He'd lost his job because of the Depression, and in order to earn money, her family rented rooms in their house to boarders like Stirling and his mother. The boarding house had been up and running for a year now. Even so, the Kittredges were only scraping by. Every month it was a struggle to find enough money to keep their *real* house, let alone to build a tree house. Still, Kit had not given up.

"I know what," said Stirling when the children finished raking. "Let's go inside and work on tree house plans."

"Okay!" said Kit and Ruthie.

Good old Stirling, thought Kit as the children and Grace trooped inside and upstairs. Stirling looked like a pipsqueak. Right now, for example, his pointy nose was so pink and frozen that it looked brittle. But Stirling was a solid friend. He drew excellent tree house plans, and he was nice about drawing *lots* of them. At Kit's request, Stirling had already drawn plans for a Tarzan tree house with swinging vines, a ship tree house with sails and a crow's nest, and a Robin Hood tree house with several levels.

Today, Ruthie had a suggestion. "How about a castle tree house?" she asked when the children were in Kit's room.

"Oh, I love that idea!" said Kit.

Ruthie was an expert on castles because she read lots of fairy tales. She was able to tell Stirling everything a castle tree house should have. Her list included battlements, round towers, banners and pennants, lookouts, curving stairways, a dungeon, and trapdoors. Stirling was just adding a drawbridge that could be raised and lowered when they heard Kit's mother calling.

"Kit, dear," she called up the stairs,

"time to set the table for dinner."

"Okay! I'm coming!" Kit answered. She turned to Ruthie and Stirling. "Let's work on the plans again tomorrow," she said. "I think this castle tree house is my most favorite of all."

Ruthie went home and Stirling hurried off to his job selling newspapers. Grace, who liked to be in the middle of things, stuck close to Kit's side and kept getting in Mother's way as they set the table.

"Grace!" scolded Mother after she had tripped over the dog for the third time. "Go away!"

Grace ambled out of the dining room. Kit and Mother could hear her settling into her favorite armchair in the living room.

"Oh, that *dog*," said Mother, with fondness and exasperation. "Well, for the time being, Grace can go right ahead and drool and shed on the chairs as much as she likes. I've got a plan to reupholster them with old curtain material." Mother looked at Kit. "Actually, my plan depends on you, Kit," she said. "My friend Beatrice Pew knows how to reupholster. She's willing to help me redo our living room chairs in exchange for using some of the curtain material on her own chairs. But she has three small children—the

twins and baby Betty. Someone needs to look after them at her house in the afternoons while she helps me here for a week or so. Could you?"

"Uh, sure," said Kit, after a split second of hesitation. She knew Mrs. Pew's three children. Baby Betty was at the wet-diaper, weepy-wailing, runny-nose stage. The twins, Dottie and Spence, were three-year-old terrors. But Kit could not refuse to help Mother.

"Thanks," said Mother. "Mrs. Pew said that we could start after school tomorrow."

"Okay," said Kit, sounding a lot more enthusiastic than she felt. *It's too bad that castle tree house doesn't exist,* she thought.

If it did, I'd put the Pew kids in the dungeon and pull up the drawbridge so they couldn't get out.

Baby-sitting for Mrs. Pew's children the next day was not as bad as Kit had thought it would be. It was worse.

First of all, Mrs. Pew insisted that her house be kept spotless. Kit was constantly chasing after Dottie and Spence shouting, "Don't touch that!" They ignored her, so she spent a lot of time putting things back where they belonged and wiping up things that got spilled. Kit began to suspect that baby Betty spilled things on purpose. She was *sure* that Dottie and Spence did.

Secondly, all three children were so loud. They shrieked when they were happy and howled when they were mad. Baby Betty was small, but she had a piercing screech, and she could keep it up for forty-five minutes at a stretch. By the time Mrs. Pew came home that first afternoon, Kit was completely fed up with baby Betty, Dottie, and Spence.

"I don't know how you stood it, Kit," Ruthie said sympathetically the next morning as she, Kit, and Stirling walked to school. "I've spent time with the Pee-yew kids, baby Betty-Wetty and those awful twins, Spottie and Dense. They're terrible."

"I'm just not the baby-sitting type,"

Kit admitted. "It reminds me of being a catcher in a nightmare baseball game where you're being pelted with balls from all sides, so you don't know where to turn first. The only time the kids quieted down at all was when I read to them. They like stories about ogres."

"Hmph!" snorted Ruthie. "Probably picking up hints. How much longer do you have to baby-sit for those kids?"

"It'll be about a week until Mother and Mrs. Pew finish all their chairs," said Kit. "I'll be glad when this home improvement project ends."

"Yeah," said Ruthie. "It'll be a big improvement for you to be home instead of at the Pews'. Then we'll have some time to do fun things again, like plan tree houses."

"Right," sighed Kit, thinking wistfully of the castle tree house.

For the next few days, Kit trudged home in the dusky fall twilight, worn out from her long afternoons with the tiresome children. She never had time to be outside after school anymore, not even to rake leaves. She had to head straight from the front door to the kitchen to help Mother get dinner ready. Kit's only reward was seeing how delighted Mother was with the spruced-up chairs. "Such an improvement!" Mother said after two of her chairs had been re-covered. And the home improvement fever was catching. Kit noticed that Dad and Stirling seemed to be working together on something in the garage. She assumed they were building a new roof for the chicken coop. Kit was glad to see Stirling and Dad so absorbed and happy. They came to dinner smiling, smelling of sawdust. Dad loved to build, and Stirling . . . Well, Stirling's father had disappeared, so Kit thought it was nice for Stirling and Dad to be friends.

One day Kit walked home just as the sun was setting. She was in good spirits because she had finally found a way to make the Pew kids behave. She told them stories she had made up about three ogres named Betty, Dottie, and Spence. They loved the stories! The

more bloody and gruesome, the better. Even baby Betty, who couldn't possibly have understood, sat quietly on Kit's lap and clapped whenever Dottie and Spence did. *It just goes to show you that imagination and ingenuity can make almost anything better,* thought Kit, *even baby-sitting.*

As Kit walked up her driveway, she was surprised to see Stirling and Dad waiting for her. Ruthie was there, too, which was unusual. "What's up?" Kit asked her.

"I don't know," Ruthie answered. "Stirling told me to come over."

Dad and Stirling shared a grin, then Dad announced, "Stirling and I have a surprise for you, Kit. We thought Ruthie would like to see it, too." He sounded pleased as punch. "Cover your eyes. You, too, Ruthie."

Kit heard the energy and enthusiasm in Dad's voice. She saw that Stirling's eyes were sparkling with excitement. Her good spirits rose even higher. She and Ruthie cheerfully shrugged at each other, covered their eyes, and let Dad and Stirling lead them to the backyard.

"You can look now," said Dad. "Ta da! We built you a tree house!"

Kit looked. She gasped. She could not believe her eyes.

Dad went on, "You've been such a good sport about baby-sitting, we wanted to make this for you as a surprise!"

"We built it partly in the garage so

you wouldn't see," added Stirling. "Then today, we finished it in the tree."

Kit's heart thudded. Tears pricked her eyes. She wanted to shout, "NO!" But she was frozen silent because *the tree house was terrible.* Everything about it was wrong. It was too close to the ground. It was too small. It was clunky and awkward. It was made of bits and pieces of mismatched wood hodge-podged together. It had none of the wonderful, imaginative features she and Ruthie and Stirling had talked about. It looked—Kit swallowed hard—like a doghouse glued on a branch. It certainly was not a castle.

Luckily, Dad and Stirling seemed to

think that Kit was speechless with happiness. Ruthie, however, was not fooled. As they all climbed into the tree house, Ruthie rushed to the rescue and talked a lot to cover up Kit's silence. "Wow!" Ruthie gushed. "What a surprise! Where'd you get the wood?"

"From a boarded-up store on the corner where I sell newspapers," Stirling explained. "They're opening a second-hand clothing store in there. When they pulled this wood off the big windows, they said I could have it."

"Wow!" said Ruthie again. She poked Kit.

"Wow," Kit echoed weakly. Ruthie poked her again. "Thanks," Kit managed to say. She mustered up a wobbly smile for Stirling and a shaky hug for Dad.

"You're welcome, sweetie," said Dad, sounding happy and satisfied. "Well, it's getting dark. We'd better go inside. Tomorrow is Saturday, and you can help us put on the finishing touches then." He and Stirling climbed down the pitiful ladder to the ground.

"You two go on ahead," said Ruthie. "Kit and I want to stay here for a minute." Ruthie made it sound as if the tree house were so fantastic, they could not tear themselves away.

The girls watched Dad and Stirling

cross the yard to the house, Dad's arm draped over Stirling's shoulders in a comfortable, buddy-buddy way.

"Oh, Kit," Ruthie whispered with heartfelt sympathy. "This is not at all the tree house you wanted, is it?"

"No," wailed Kit. "I mean, I knew towers and a dungeon were unrealistic, but this . . . This is awful. And I can't think of any way to make it look better."

"Well, maybe a blindfold," Ruthie said, gently joking.

"I hate it," said Kit. "I know that Dad and Stirling want me to say that I love it. What am I going to do?"

"If they ask how you like it, there's only one thing to do," said Ruthie.

"What?" asked Kit.

"Lie," Ruthie replied.

It looks terrible even in the moonlight, Kit thought. She was sitting by the window in her room, gloomily looking down at the disappointing tree house. Kit sighed. Was Ruthie right? Should she just lie? Kit shifted uncomfortably. Or could she possibly tell Dad and Stirling very politely that their tree house was not quite what she'd had in mind and ask them to take it apart and rebuild it so that it was closer to what she wanted? As Kit stared at the tree house, she thought she saw a light flickering inside it. Then the light disappeared. Kit leaned forward, her nose pressed to the window. There it was again! Curious, Kit pulled on her slippers, tiptoed downstairs, grabbed her coat, ran outside across the dew-wet grass, and climbed up into the tree house.

Stirling was there, holding Kit's lantern. "Hi," he said.

"Hi," said Kit. "I saw the light, and I—"

"Listen," Stirling interrupted earnestly. "You didn't fool me. I know you don't like this tree house. The truth is, I knew all along that you weren't going to like it. But . . ." Stirling's low voice got even lower. "It was just so great to be working with your dad, I didn't want to say anything." Stirling looked at Kit. "How about you?" he asked. "Are you going to tell your dad that you hate the tree house, or are you going to settle for it?"

"I don't know," said Kit. "I don't mind settling for things like old winter coats that are too small, or even giving up afternoons to baby-sit for ogres. But my tree house . . . I didn't want to give up on that."

Stirling nodded.

A breeze blew through the tree house. Kit heard paper rustle. She looked at the wall and saw that Stirling had tacked up some of the old tree house plans. The light of the lantern danced across the Tarzan tree house plans, the ship tree house plans, the Robin Hood tree house plans, and the castle tree house plans. "Stirling!" said Kit. "Why'd you put these up? They just remind me of how disappointed I am. I want to forget them."

"I don't think you should," said Stirling. "I don't think you should give up on any of your plans or dreams, no matter how things are right now."

Kit took a deep, shaky breath. She smelled the sharp, turpentiny scent of the wood and felt its roughness under her hand. She listened to the scritch-scratch of the branches tapping gently against the roof and saw the way the

moonlight sneaked through the cracks between the boards. She knew Dad would have built her a castle in the air if he could have, but all he had was time, scraps, and love.

"I was thinking," Stirling said quietly, "maybe we could hang a rope ladder out the back."

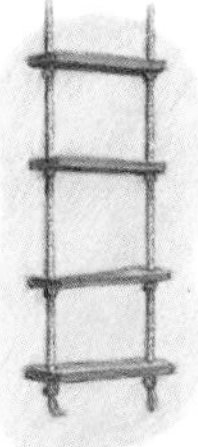

"It'll take more than a rope ladder to improve this tree house," Kit said. "I'm not sure that even imagination and ingenuity can make it better." She sighed. "It's a terrible tree house, but I love Dad too much to tell him, so I guess I'm stuck with it." She turned and looked at the plan for the castle tree house, then she grinned at Stirling. "At least *right now*."

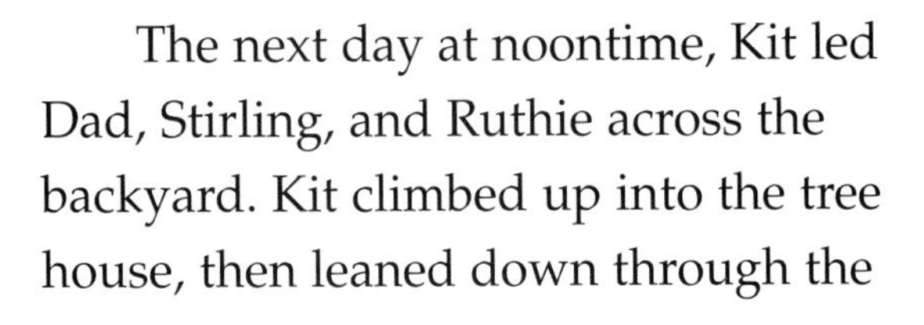

The next day at noontime, Kit led Dad, Stirling, and Ruthie across the backyard. Kit climbed up into the tree house, then leaned down through the

"Come on up. This time I have a surprise for you."

hole in the floor and beckoned to them, saying, "Come on up. This time *I* have a surprise for *you*."

"Wow!" said Ruthie with genuine enthusiasm as she popped up through the hole. Dad and Stirling followed close behind her, and all three admired the curtains Kit had put up and the picnic lunch she'd set out on a tablecloth with matching napkins.

"Mother's going to help me make pillows, too," said Kit. "I'm using the old material that came off the chairs she reupholstered."

"Very ingenious," said Dad. He leaned back, looked around the tree house, and smiled. "This is great," he said happily. "Isn't it?"

Ruthie and Stirling both looked hard at Kit.

Kit grinned. "Yes," she agreed with her whole heart. "It is."

Meet the Author

Valerie Tripp

At 9 Now

I used to climb the big maple tree in our front yard and daydream about fancy tree houses, just like Kit. Now my daughter has a tree platform way up in a pine tree. It's not a castle, but it does have a rope ladder!

Valerie Tripp has written forty-seven books in The American Girls Collection, including eight about Kit.

A Peek Into the Past

Houses in 1934

Kit longed for a tree house, a place of her own perched high above the hustle and bustle of her family's boarding house.

Children growing up during the Depression learned to value private places because most children shared their homes with many other people. Sharing

No space was wasted in a house filled with people.

living space was a way to save money at a time when money was scarce.

In the early 1930s, households expanded as relatives and friends moved in together. One girl called her grandparents' home the "rubber house" because of the way it seemed to stretch to fit so many people—first the girl's own family, and then her uncle and cousins, too. The house had only two bedrooms, but it fit five adults and six children!

Households also grew when families took in *boarders,* or paying guests, as the Kittredges did. Boarders paid by the week or the month for a place to sleep and for meals. Many families were able to keep their homes because they used money from boarders to pay the monthly *mortgage,* the amount they owed the bank for their home loan. Boarders benefited, too, because boarding with a family was less expensive than renting an apartment.

Unfortunately, families didn't always have enough room in their homes to fit extra people comfortably. Bedrooms had to be shared and new rooms created. Some families converted porches and attics into bedrooms. Other families made bedrooms in their basements, where there was plenty of room but little privacy. Bedspreads were hung on clotheslines to separate girls' "rooms" from boys'.

Some boarding houses charged seven dollars a week.

Bathrooms had to be shared, too—some by as many as 15 people! Some families added an extra bathroom in the basement or attic or used an old outhouse. One woman remembers sharing an attic bathroom with another family. The bathtub sat in the middle of the floor, with no walls around it, so using the tub felt like "taking a bath on Main Street." Bathers sang loudly to keep "intruders" away!

Sharing space with so many people was especially difficult for children, who often had to give up their bedrooms to paying guests. Children in large households had extra chores to

If the bathtub was full, a washtub had to do.

The days of pretending to cook and clean were over. Now girls had real work to do!

do, too, such as laundry and cooking. But children knew that extra people meant extra income—money their families needed to keep their homes.

Many families that couldn't afford to pay the mortgage were *evicted*, or thrown out of their homes. If they had nowhere else to go, they created houses out of packing crates, cardboard, old car bodies,

Hoovervilles sprang up in vacant lots.

or piano boxes. Groups of these houses were called "Hoovervilles" after former president Herbert Hoover, who many felt hadn't done much to end the Depression.

Other homeless families moved from one place to the next. "Home" one night might be a soup kitchen, where family members were fed and sometimes allowed to sleep. The next night, they might be sleeping in a tent in a hobo *jungle,* or camp, near the railroad tracks.

In the winter, some people even lived in caves dug out of the earth.

Children who saw people living in makeshift homes learned not to complain about their own cramped homes. Instead, they made do with the space they had and—with a little creativity and imagination—made it their own.

A crowded attic becomes a circus tent!

An American Girls Pastime

Make a Jewelry Tree

"Spruce" up your room!

Girls in Kit's time found inexpensive ways to decorate their rooms. They made use of natural materials, like flowers, leaves, and pinecones, which were easy to find—and free! The best crafts were also functional, like this mini tree with lots of branches for storing jewelry.

Gather a few outdoor treasures, and make a tiny tree of your own. Slide rings onto the short upper branches, dangle necklaces from the middle branches, and tuck bracelets around the base of the tree!

YOU WILL NEED:

An adult to help you

5-inch clay flowerpot

Newspaper

Acrylic paints

Foam paintbrush

Duct tape

Clean, dry branch (2 to 2½ feet tall)

4 small pinecones

Enamel or floral spray paint, glossy white

1½ pounds plaster of Paris

2 bricks or wooden blocks

2 oz. Spanish moss (found at most craft stores)

Thin gold cord

Scissors

Small artificial bird

Craft glue

1. Wipe the dust off the flowerpot and place it on newspaper. Paint the pot, including the top rim, with acrylic paint. Let dry 10 minutes. Paint a second coat if needed.

2. Use duct tape to cover the hole in the bottom of the pot.

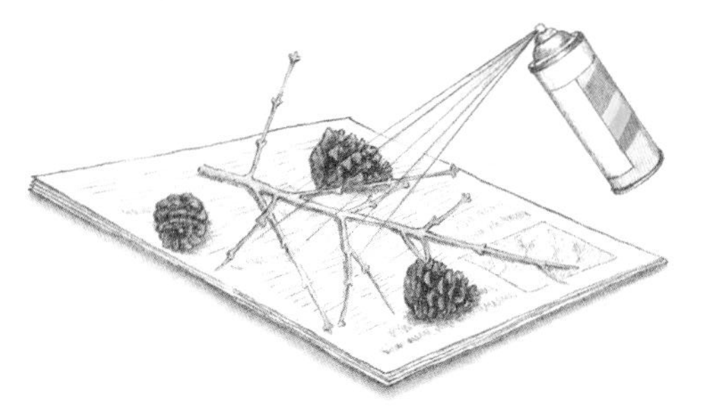

3. Lay the branch and pinecones on newspaper in a well-ventilated area. Have an adult help you paint them with the spray paint using quick, short strokes. Let dry 30 minutes.

4. Mix the plaster of Paris according to package instructions.

Step 5 *Step 6*

5. Hold the branch in the center of the pot. Have an adult help you pour the plaster into the pot, filling it about three-fourths full.

6. Lay blocks or bricks across the top of the pot, on both sides of the branch. The blocks will help keep the branch straight. Let the plaster set overnight.

Step 7 *Step 8*

7. Arrange moss around the base of the tree. Lay pinecones on top of the moss, or use gold cord to hang them from the tree.

8. Glue the bird to a tuft of moss, and place a "nest" on a branch. Now add jewelry to complete your tree!